W9-BLF-414

CYNTHIA RYLANT

Mr. Putter & Tabby
Hit the Slope

Illustrated by

ARTHUR HOWARD

Houghton Mifflin Harcourt

Boston New York

The illustrations in this book were done in pencil, watercolor,
and gouache on 250-gram cotton rag paper.
The text type was set in Berkeley Old Style Book.
The display type was set in Artcraft.

Library of Congress Cataloging-in-Publication Data is available.
ISBN 978-0-15-206427-3

Manufactured in China
SCP 1 3 5 7 9 10 8 6 4 2
4500596465

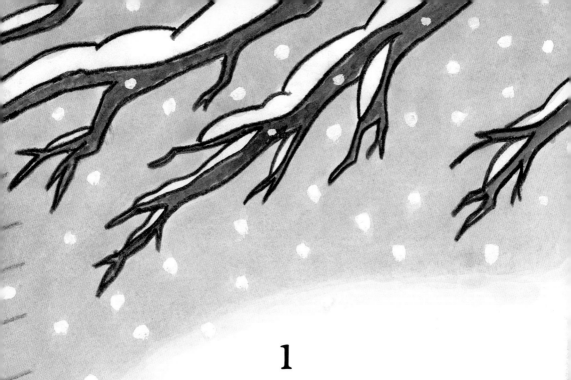

1

Slow

Mr. Putter and his fine cat, Tabby,
liked winter.
But sometimes things were
a little slow.

There were no tulips to tend.

There were no berries to pick.

The hammock was under

three feet of snow.

"We need some fun,"
said Mr. Putter to Tabby.

He thought and thought.
What is fun in the winter?
Then he remembered.

2

The Best Fun

When Mr. Putter was a boy,
he had a red sled
with silver runners.
And *that* was the best fun
of all in the winter.

He would go to the top
of the highest hill.
He would shout, "COWABUNGA!"
And down that hill he would fly.

He was a very good sledder.
He gave other people rides.

Winter was not slow in those days.

Mr. Putter thought,

Why should winter be slow in these days?

He called Mrs. Teaberry.

3

The Slope

Of course Mrs. Teaberry had sleds.
Mrs. Teaberry had *everything*.
She lived next door
with her good dog, Zeke,
and they were always prepared.
One look in the garage said so.

Mr. Putter called Mrs. Teaberry,
and the next thing he knew,
he was on a slope in his mittens.
He had a lot more than just mittens on.

Tabby was wearing a sweater
Mrs. Teaberry had knitted her for Christmas.
It was a little itchy,
which made Tabby a little twitchy.
Her tail was *very* twitchy.
But she was warm.

Mrs. Teaberry and Zeke
were dressed for the Alps.

Mr. Putter looked at them and said,
"You are dressed for the Alps."

Mrs. Teaberry was very adventurous.

Mr. Putter liked that about her.

His adventures mostly came

on a porch with a book.

That is, until Mrs. Teaberry.

Mr. Putter looked
down the slope.
He was ready.

4

Like a Rocket

Mr. Putter wanted Tabby to ride
the sled with him.
Tabby was not so sure.
Her tail was very, *very* twitchy.
Mr. Putter tried to put her on the sled.
He thought she would like it.

Tabby was not liking it.

Then Zeke jumped on the sled with Tabby.
And that was that.

The next thing Mr. Putter knew,

he had no sled,

no cat,

and no fun.

Fun was already halfway down the slope.

"Hop on!" shouted Mrs. Teaberry.
Mr. Putter did not want to hop on.
He wanted his own sled.

But he hopped on anyway.

"COWABUNGA!" shouted Mrs. Teaberry.

Mr. Putter and Mrs. Teaberry flew
down that slope like a rocket.

They caught up with the other sled.
Mr. Putter and Mrs. Teaberry
looked over at Tabby and Zeke.
Tabby and Zeke looked over
at Mr. Putter and Mrs. Teaberry.
"Good dog, Zeke!" called Mrs. Teaberry.

Zeke wagged.

He was happy.

Tabby twitched.

She was not.

Mr. Putter just held on.

5

Muffins and Cream

Everyone came to a stop
at the bottom of the slope.
Tabby jumped off the sled
and went up a tree.
She would not come down
until Mr. Putter promised her
muffins and cream.
Then she came down.

When Mr. Putter and Tabby went home,
they took off their wet clothes.
They had a warm bath.

They had muffins and cream.

A day on the slope

had worn them out.

So they curled up together
in Mr. Putter's chair.
They closed their eyes.
And no one twitched.

DATE DUE

PRINTED IN U.S.A.